Other books in
THE TIME WARP TRIO series

HATSHEPSUT

THE TIME WARP TRIO

TUT, TUT

by Jon Scieszka

illustrated by Lane Smith

VIKING

With special thanks to Catharine Roehrig, Associate Curator, Egyptian Art, Metropolitan Museum of Art.

VIKING
Published by the Penguin Group
Penguin Books USA Inc., 375 Hudson Street, New York, New York 10014, U.S.A.
Penguin Books Ltd, 27 Wrights Lane, London W8 5TZ, England
Penguin Books Australia Ltd, Ringwood, Victoria, Australia
Penguin Books Canada Ltd, 10 Alcorn Avenue, Toronto, Ontario, Canada M4V 3B2
Penguin Books (N.Z.) Ltd, 182-190 Wairau Road, Auckland 10, New Zealand

Penguin Books Ltd, Registered Offices: Harmondsworth, Middlesex, England

First published in 1996 by Viking, a division of Penguin Books USA Inc.

1 3 5 7 9 10 8 6 4 2

Text copyright © Jon Scieszka, 1996
Illustrations copyright © Lane Smith, 1996
All rights reserved

ISBN 0-670-84832-8

Printed in U.S.A.
Set in Sabon

For the fifth grade
Egyptologists of
The Berkeley Carroll School

ONE

I opened the door to my room and saw a terrible scene. A giant woman stood in King Tut's tomb. An even bigger cat crouched just behind it.

"Anna!" I yelled. "What are you doing?"

Sam and Fred pushed into the room behind me.

"She's wrecking our ancient Egypt projects," said Fred. He tossed an extra figure out of his diorama. "Ms. B. would kill me if she found G. I. Joe in my 'Making of a Mummy.'"

Sam picked up another action figure. "I'm sure she'd love Spiderman in my Book of the Dead scroll and Barbie in Joe's 'King Tut's Tomb.'"

"That is not Barbie. It's the goddess Isis," said Anna.

"I didn't know Isis wore high heels," I said. "And would you please get that stupid cat away from the tomb. She's licking the burial chamber."

Anna took the cat and her doll and settled them

both in her lap. "Cleo is not a stupid cat and she wasn't licking your stupid burial chamber. She was helping Isis stop the evil grave robbers from breaking into the Queen Pharaoh's tomb."

"You are such a pain," I said. "And that shows how much you know about ancient Egypt. Only kings were Pharaohs. They never had women Pharaohs."

I wiped the cat slobber off my model of King Tut's tomb.

"Oh yes, they did," said Anna.

"Oh no, they didn't," I said, doing my most annoying imitation of Anna's voice.

"Well, who is this then?" said Anna. She opened one of the books on my desk and pointed to a picture.

Sam adjusted his glasses and leaned over to take

a closer look. "Now *that's* the goddess Isis. You can tell because she has that thing that looks like a chair on her head. And there's that same throne shape in the hieroglyph next to her. That's her cartouche signature thing."

"Pharaohs are usually depicted wearing the white crown of Upper Egypt and/or the red crown of Lower Egypt," said Fred in his fake teacher voice. He flipped up the bill of his baseball cap. "Only the most awesome Pharaohs wore the Blue Jay crown of Toronto."

"But I saw a picture of a woman wearing the two Pharaoh crowns," said Anna.

"I'll bet you your week's allowance you didn't," I said.

"I'll bet you I did," said Anna, putting Cleo down and looking through the pile of Egypt books.

"And you have to clean the kitty litter for my week, too," I added.

Sam drew a few more teeth on the figure of the Devourer in the Weighing of the Heart scene in his scroll, then stood back to admire all three projects.

"Congratulations Trio," said Sam. "Here we have three excellent projects on ancient Egypt, finished one whole day before they are due, and nobody even mentioned using a certain *Book* to help us with our research."

Fred turned his Blue Jays cap inside out and balanced it upside down on his head. "We must be getting smart."

"I wouldn't go that far," said Sam.

"I'm still time-lagged from our last adventure," I said. "Plus, I promised I wouldn't use *The Book* again until I've figured out every tip and rule in there."

"Aha!" yelled Anna. "Here it is."

Cleo jumped on the desk and rubbed her cheek on the book Anna held.

"I found it. A picture of a lady wearing both

crowns." Anna held up a thin blue book with twisting silver designs.

A faint green mist began to form on the sugar-cube steps of King Tut's tomb.

"No!" screamed Fred, Sam, and I in unison. Fred and I dove for *The Book*. Sam dove for the door. We met in mid-jump and ended up in a pile on the floor.

"Yes it is," said Anna. She scratched Cleo's head and studied the picture in *The Book*. "See there's the white crown—"

"I don't want to be a mummy," moaned Sam in the gathering green cloud.

"—and there's the red crown."

A flower of dense green fog bloomed and covered *Book*, sister, and cat.

"Here we go again," said Fred.

Then the fog swallowed us, and we were gone.

TWO

Now before things get out of hand (and you know they will as soon as we land), I'd like to take a minute to explain a few things.

First of all—I had no idea what I was getting into when my uncle Joe gave me *The Book* for my birthday. It turns out that this is no ordinary book. This thing is a time machine. Every time we open it, it takes us to a different time. Which sounds like great fun. But there is one little problem. The only way to get back to our time is to find *The Book* in the other time. And whenever we time travel, *The Book* has a nasty habit of disappearing.

We've gotten in trouble looking for *The Book* in King Arthur's court, on Blackbeard's pirate ship, in a stone-age cave, and in places you don't even want to know about.

So you would think by now we would have figured out how to use *The Book* without losing it.

Well . . . we haven't. And if you've got any bright ideas of what we should do—keep them to yourself.

Sorry if I sound a little cranky. But this disappearing *Book* thing is starting to get on my nerves. I swore to Sam and Fred that I would figure out *The Book* before it took us on any more time travels. Then my wonderful sister had to go and get us in the same mess again. I may just have to ask my mom about *The Book* straight out. She gave it to Uncle Joe, and I have a sneaking feeling she knows more than she's telling.

If you've read any of the Time Warp Trio's other adventures, you know as well as I do what's coming next. We're bound to land in some kind of trouble. Except this time I have the added worry of keeping track of a little sister and her cat, too. Great.

Wish me luck and turn the page. I'll bet you your allowance and a week of kitty-litter cleaning that we end up in King Tut's tomb . . . or someplace worse.

THREE

For all of the times we've time warped, I've never gotten used to it. It's like dreaming you're falling, floating in the ocean, and spinning in one of those awful teacup rides at the carnival all at once. You get large. You get small. You get curved. Then you are you again.

When the Time Warp teacup ride finally stopped, Fred, Sam, and I found ourselves in the same heap we had been in 1996. But the dusty stone floor and the strange light weren't anything like my room in 1996.

Fred adjusted his Blue Jays cap and jumped to his feet. "Check this out. Statues, paintings, hieroglyphics. We must be back in King Tut's tomb."

"Surprise, surprise," said Sam, still sitting in the middle of the floor. "And let me guess—*The Book* is nowhere in sight."

I looked around the small stone room. A group

of statues and things stood jumbled in the corner near Fred. There was no *Book*, and no little sister Anna or her cat Cleo.

"Don't panic,". I said. "This time we'll make a plan. *The Book* is usually nearby. So we find Anna, find *The Book*, and warp back out of here before we get in any trouble."

"Great plan, fearless leader," said Sam. "Only I'm not moving from this spot, because I would like to keep my hands."

Fred came over with a gold cobra crown wrapped around his hat. "We're rich! We've finally hit pay dirt with that freaky *Book*. Real treasure."

"What do you mean—you want to keep your hands?" I asked Sam.

"You junior Egyptologists seem to have forgotten," lectured Sam, "that the authorities usually punished grave robbers by chopping off their hands. So I'm staying right here. No one is going to call me a grave robber."

Fred went back to the statues. "Oh come on, you chicken. They won't miss a few gold pieces."

I looked at Sam, sitting on his hands. I looked at Fred, digging in a dead person's treasure. "Are you both nuts? Fred, get away from that stuff.

Sam, get on your feet. We are going to find *The Book*, find my sister and her cat, and get out of here before—"

A loud crash echoed in the hallway outside. More lights flickered. An angry voice yelled.

"My hands," squeaked Sam, folding them under his armpits.

"Yikes," said Fred, trying to yank the cobra off his cap.

The sound of the voice grew louder.

"They're headed this way," I whispered. "Hide."

We ran in circles looking for something, anything, to hide behind. The three of us saw the statues in the corner and all had the same idea. We jumped behind the statues and froze into a pose, just as bright torchlight flooded the room.

A pudgy, bald man in a white robe and sandals held the torch and a whippy stick that he swished around in the air at two taller guys dragging a big painted trunk.

"You idiots. I can't believe I ever offered you a place in eternal life. Your mother must have been a blind hippo and your father a three-legged donkey. If anything is broken in there I'll—"

At this the nasty little guy started slashing his

11

whip around like he was battling a whole army.

"Yes, your grace," said the one in a white skirt.

"Thank you, your grace," said the other.

"Bring the rest into the next room. And if you break one tiny amulet or shawabti, I'll make sure the gods keep you paddling a barge in the flaming lakes of Duat forever. Now go!"

The two guys hustled off and left their leader standing over the treasure. I had no idea who this guy was, but the strange look in his eye made me think he was up to no good. Then he started talking to himself like evil guys in movies always

do, and I *knew* he was up to no good.

"My plan works to perfection. As soon as the Pharaoh's temple is completed, *my* temple will be completed. These secret rooms and treasures will give me power greater than any Pharaoh in the next life. All will remember and revere my name— the great priest Hatsnat."

Fred shot me a look. If he was thinking what I was thinking, we could have sworn the guy had said his name was Hot Snot. I had just convinced myself it couldn't be, when he started up again.

"Great Hatsnat. Most Awesome Hatsnat. The Wonder of All, Hatsnat." The little bald guy paced around the room, trying out his different names. Fred, Sam, and I bit our lips, trying not to burst out laughing.

He walked to the doorway and turned for one last look at his treasure. We were almost safe. Then he said, "The Grand, Glorious Most Awesome Wonder of All . . . Hatsnat."

That did it. Fred snorted out a laugh.

Hatsnat jumped three feet into the air.

Sam and I couldn't hold it in any longer. We fell on the floor laughing. We had just barely managed to stop howling, when Hatsnat held his torch toward us. "Thieves. How dare you defile the temple of Hatsnat."

Have you ever been someplace where you're not supposed to laugh, but you just can't help it? That's exactly where we were.

"Hot Snot?" I laughed.

"Cold Boogers," laughed Fred.

"Not robbers," laughed Sam.

We laughed so hard we could hardly breathe.

Hatsnat did not look amused. In fact, he looked mad enough to kill.

FOUR

Once we stopped laughing, it finally sunk in that we were in serious trouble. Hatsnat lined us up against the wall, twitching his whip.

"Thieves. Vermin. Crocodile dung. Where do you robbers come from in these strange garments and sandals? Answer!"

Sam was the first to recover and jump into quick-talking action. "Robbers? No sir. We're not robbers. We come from . . . umm . . . another land. But we are not robbers." Sam shoved his hands deep in his pockets. "Not us. No way."

Hatsnat slashed his whip through the air. "Then how did you get into this secret room?"

"Would you believe magic?" said Fred.

Hatsnat leaned back, suddenly looking a teeny bit afraid. "Magic? You are followers of Isis? You have powers beyond this life?"

"Yeah, kind of," said Fred. Then he suddenly

pushed me forward. "Joe here is actually the most powerful magician in our land."

"Thanks, Fred," I said and punched him in the arm as hard as I could.

Hatsnat tapped the end of his whip on his chin. "Magicians, you say? Hmmm. Then conjure me jewels, elephant tusks, a live baboon."

I couldn't believe I was on the spot again. For a guy who's not even an official card-carrying magician, I sure get an awful lot of work. I wracked my brain for a good trick.

"Jewels and monkeys? That's baby stuff. I can perform wonders you've never dreamed of," I said, stalling for time. "But first I need a few things. Do you have a thin blue book? About this big? With silver designs on the front and back? It's kind of a book of how things work in our land."

"Instructions for the afterlife?" said Hatsnat. He took a small package wrapped in linen from the trunk and handed it to me.

I couldn't believe we had found *The Book* this easily. Finally our luck was changing.

"Great," I said. "Now stand back." I un-wrapped the linen and took out . . . a scroll of drawings and hieroglyphics. Our luck was definitely changing. Changing for the worse.

Sam groaned. "That's a book for the afterlife all right. It's a Book of the Dead. Which is exactly what we're going to be if you don't show the nice man some magic, Joe."

"Thank you so much for your assistance, Magician Sam," I said. Then I saw a small scrap of papyrus about the size of a dollar bill, and I remembered a classic trick. "Allow me to show you that we magicians are faster than any man," I said to Hatsnat. I held the papyrus piece in my left hand, between the open thumb and finger of my right hand.

"I drop the papyrus. I catch it between my thumb and finger. I drop it. I catch it. Easy, yes?"

Hatsnat nodded.

"Then let's see if you are as fast as a magician. I'll drop it. You catch it."

Hatsnat held out his thumb and forefinger. I placed

17

the papyrus between them and asked, "Ready?"

"Of course."

I dropped the papyrus. He missed by a mile.

"I wasn't ready."

I dropped it again. He missed again.

"The light is dim."

Missed again.

"Something was in my eye."

Not even close.

"Enough!" Hatsnat sliced the air with his whip. He was still mad, but you could tell he was looking at us differently. I figured I'd better keep him guessing while I had him believing us.

"Another simple challenge." I put the piece of papyrus on the floor about two feet away from the wall. "Stand with your heels against the wall. Bend over and pick up the papyrus without moving your feet."

Hatsnat frowned. "That is simple for a great priest. Here, hold the torch."

Hatsnat placed his heels against the wall, bent forward, and just about fell on his face. "I wasn't truly trying." Hatsnat started again, bending slowly forward. Sam and Fred gave me the thumbs-up sign. Hatsnat staggered.

"So you see we really are magicians," said Sam. "We're not robbers."

"Yeah," said Fred. "We thought this was King Tut's tomb. We didn't even know that it was your secret room in the Pharaoh's temple."

Hatsnat's eyes narrowed to little slits. This did not seem like a good thing. "Yes, you do know this is my secret room, don't you?"

"Oh, but don't worry," said Sam. "We won't tell anyone, really."

"Really," said Hatsnat. "No, I guess you won't." He rubbed his bald head and gave us a funny look. "Well, what am I thinking? The Pharaoh would be very angry with me if I did not welcome such great magicians with the proper gifts. Come with me."

Hatsnat led us out the doorway and through a maze of hallways left and right, up and down, and back around. The walls were covered with brightly colored carvings of gods and goddesses. I spotted my personal favorite—Thoth, the ibis-headed god of writing.

We slipped through a gap in the stone wall and came out behind a curtain into a huge room with statues, jars, crowns, and a million pieces sparkling with gold and jewels. Suddenly Hatsnat was our best friend.

"Take whatever you desire," he said. "The Pharoah's treasure is your treasure."

Fred picked up a miniature gold mummy coffin.

Hatsnat helped Sam with a falcon-shaped neck piece bigger than him.

I couldn't decide between a gold statue of Osiris and a great-looking dagger.

"Nice work with the paper tricks," whispered Fred. "You definitely faked him out."

"A little knowledge of reflexes and the human body's center of gravity," I said modestly. "No one can do those things, but he doesn't know that." I tried on a few scarab rings.

Sam folded a crook and flail across his jeweled chest. "King Sam."

"But how come he speaks English?" said Fred. "Or do we understand Egyptian?"

"There's always some kind of instant translation thing that happens in all of the time travel books I've ever read," said Sam. "Because if they didn't have that, none of the characters would understand what each other was saying."

"Oh," said Fred.

I settled on the dagger and an ankh symbol necklace. "Yeah, I'll have to look that up in *The Book* when we find it."

"Do us all a favor," said Sam, adjusting his new Pharaoh beard. "Don't."

We were so busy talking and comparing treasures that none of us noticed Hatsnat edging toward an outer doorway. Out of the corner of my eye I saw him suddenly push over a huge statue. I thought he'd gone crazy. The giant stone nose smashed off the statue's face with a deafening crash

as it hit the floor. We froze as we heard the sounds of shouts and running. We saw Hatsnat smile one awful smile. Then I understood. But it was too late.

Hatsnat leaned out the doorway and yelled, "Thieves! Robbers! Help! They smash the Pharaoh's very image! Help! Help!"

In a matter of minutes we were caught red-handed. Strong Egyptian workers dragged us out into blinding daylight and tied us with our arms stretched out across a stone block.

"They are thieves," said Hatsnat. "Kill them."

"Wait a minute," said Sam. "Can't we discuss this? Let's not be so hasty."

Hatsnat paused. "You're right." He turned to the guard holding his very large sword over our heads. "Let's not be so hasty. First, chop off their hands. Then chop off their heads."

FIVE

When someone is about to die in a book, they usually say "their life flashed before them." The only thing that flashed before me was that my mom was going to be awfully mad at me for losing my sister in ancient Egypt.

Hatsnat laughed at his own bad joke. His guard raised his sword. And we were about to become the Time Warp No-Hands Trio when someone yelled.

"Hatsnat! Hold that sword. What terrible ritual is this at the entrance to the Pharaoh's temple?"

"They are robbers, sire. We caught them stealing treasure and smashing statues."

"Stand them before me."

The guards untied us and dragged us in front of a boy in a white robe.

"Bow before the king," said the big brute with the sword. He looked disappointed at having missed a chance to chop off a few body parts.

Sam adjusted his glasses. "What king? I don't see any king." The guard whacked Sam across the back with the flat of his sword.

"There in front of you, worm. Now bow."

"Hey, lay off the sword work there, big boy," said Fred. "If you want to mess with someone, bring it on." Fred raised his hands and got into his fighting stance.

I decided I would like to keep my hands and head attached to my body, so I jumped in between them. "The Time Warp Trio, sire. At your service." I bowed to the boy in the robe. He was a guy about our age. Short black hair and a friendly look on his face. "We are three magicians who have lost our way from our world due to . . . uh . . . technical difficulties. We never meant to steal any treasure. We're just looking for one small book, one small girl, and a cat."

The boy king looked at the three of us and smiled. "Magicians? Really?" He checked out Fred's sneakers. "And those must be magic sandals."

That's when it hit me. Boy king? "Excuse me, sire. But is your name King Tut?"

"No. It's Thutmose," said the king. "Thutmose III to be exact. Someday I will be the greatest

24

king of all. But can I try those on? What can they do?" So he wasn't King Tut, but he was crazy for Fred's basketball sneakers.

Fred swapped shoes for sandals with the king. "These will give you the power to drive the lane and sky to the hoop. Here, let me show you." Fred made a quick hoop by sticking a loop of reed in a crack in the stone wall, then he passed me a pomegranate from one of the worker's lunches. I shot a quick jumper right through it.

"Yes!" said Sam in his best Marv Albert imitation.

In half a second we were running all over the temple steps showing the king reverse layups, three-sixty spins, and windmill jams. Thutmose was a natural.

"The Pharaoh is deep in the corner," said Sam into a handy papyrus-branch microphone.

"The shot clock is down to three. He fakes left, drives right, and slams home the pomegranate to win it at the buzzer!"

Thutmose slapped Fred a high-five and we sat down. It was then that we noticed Hatsnat looking completely bent out of shape.

"Sire, these three are thieves. The law says we must deal with them severely."

"Oh, take it easy, Hatsnat," said Thutmose. "These are not thieves. These are my friends." Fred, Sam, and I smiled.

"Yeah. Chill out there, Warm Goober," said Sam. "We're hanging with the king."

Hatsnat did his eye-narrowing thing again.

"But to satisfy the law," said Thutmose, "we will bring them back to the palace. The Pharaoh can decide what must be done. After all, it is her temple where they were found."

I was confused. "But I thought *you* were the Pharaoh. Isn't this your temple?"

"I am Pharaoh and so is my aunt Hatshepsut," said Thutmose. He pointed up the huge tiers of steps and columns that disappeared back into the rock. For the first time we noticed hundreds of workers swarming all over. Some of them were carving the finishing touches on a lane of sphinxes leading up to the temple. Another line of them hauled a giant column over wooden rollers with ropes. "This is to be Hatshepsut's temple."

"There goes one week's allowance and a week of kitty-litter cleaning," I said.

"But I am the son of Thutmose II, and I will rule when I grow up," said Thutmose. He looked around, and everyone including Fred, Sam, and me naturally gave him a little bow. There was definitely something kingly about him. "To the boats everyone," he ordered. "We're going back to the palace."

Thutmose led us down from the cliffs to a broad, slow-moving river. A whole gang of attendants trailed behind. Hatsnat brought up the rear whispering something to two of his priests. I recognized them as the ones who had dropped the trunk in Hatsnat's secret room.

"I don't trust that guy," said Fred.

"Oh you can trust him," said Sam. "Since we are the only ones who know he's making his own secret room inside the Pharaoh's temple, you can trust him—to do everything he can to get rid of us."

SIX

Everyone boarded the three boats at the dock. Hatsnat joined us in the royal boat. It had one big square sail and two long steering oars along each side. We pushed off up the river against the current, leading our mini-fleet of three ships. Birds flew overhead. Palm trees and papyrus waved in the wind along the wide river.

"Wow," said Sam. "The Nile—the Perfect River."

"Yes," said Thutmose. "Though not so perfect

these days. Everyone waits and prays for the Inundation."

"Inna-what?" said Fred.

"Inundation," answered Sam. "When the Nile overflows its banks every year. That's how the fields are watered and fertilized."

"How faskinating, Professor Sam," said Fred. "And can you also tells us what methods of irrigation are used during dry periods?"

"Why yes," said Sam. "Most farmers use a system of canals and a long pole with a bucket and a counterweight called a *shaduf* to—"

Fred slapped Sam with his hat. "I was just kidding. Save it for social studies."

The captain of our boat trimmed the sail, and we picked up speed. Water gurgled off the side and curled into a wake behind us.

"This is fantastic," I said, looking out over the great river with boats of all sizes coming and going. Here was a civilization that had lasted for three thousand years. It made our two hundred years of U.S. history look like the blink of an eye.

"Yeah," said Fred, leaning over to watch our wake. "Totally fantastic. If I had a board, I'd be wake jumping and Nile surfing in a minute."

"It is a beautiful land," said Thutmose. "And when I rule, I plan to make Egypt the greatest land it has ever been. What is your land like?"

"Well the East River is a little different from the Nile," said Sam. "Not so many palm trees. More apartment buildings and highways."

"Apartment buildings? Highways?" said a familiar creepy voice. "What are those?" Hatsnat appeared, like a bad smell in a dark movie theater—no one knows where it comes from.

"That's how we magicians live," said Sam. "Houses are a hundred feet up in the air. Metal chariots go ten times faster than we're sailing now."

"Is it possible?" said Thutmose.

"Just what I was thinking, sire," said Hatsnat.

This did not make Sam happy. "You think you're such Hatsnat, why don't you—"

"Hey, what's that?" interrupted Fred.

Thutmose looked over the rail at a cluster of shapes in the water. "Hippos and crocodiles. They usually stay away from boats. With the dry weather they grow bolder looking for something to eat."

"Creatures of chaos and the god Seth is what

they are," muttered Hatsnat. "As Seth ripped the body of Osiris into pieces, so would his creatures tear us apart. Look. One swims toward us."

Sure enough, one of the thin crocodile heads was slicing through the water right for our ship. Thutmose pulled out a small blue hippo hanging on a string around his neck. "Hold up your amulets. That will chase them off."

Hatsnat held up his green crocodile amulet, then gave us that sneaky smile of his. "The great musicians have no amulets?"

"We don't need no stinking amulets," said Fred, quoting one of his favorite movies.

"Yeah," Sam chimed in. "We've got stronger magic." He dug in the pocket of his jeans, pulled out a paper clip, and held it over the rail toward the approaching crocodile.

And I'm not sure exactly what happened next. Hatsnat claimed it was an accident. One minute Thutmose, Sam, and Hatsnat were holding their amulets toward the crocodile. The next minute the boat shifted, Hatsnat fell into Sam, and Sam was over the rail and in the Nile.

The boat sailed on, leaving Sam splashing in its wake. The hungry crocodile saw the splashes

and changed his course and his dinner plans.

"Turn the boat around," I yelled.

Hatsnat rubbed his little green crocodile. "Don't worry. The great magician should be fine with his powerful amulet."

There was nothing we could do but watch in horror as our boat kept sailing, leaving Sam with nothing but a paper clip between him and one very hungry crocodile.

SEVEN

We rushed to the back of the boat.

"Man overboard," yelled Sam, splashing to keep his head above water.

The crocodile closed in. Hatsnat rubbed his amulet and licked his thin lips.

"Throw him a line," yelled Fred.

We ran around like crazy men, looking for something to throw to Sam. But there was no rope. The oars were lashed tight. The only loose thing on deck was a long wooden coffin. Fred and I tried to pick it up and throw it overboard. We could barely lift it an inch.

Sam's head grew smaller and the crocodile head sped closer to him as we sailed away. A merchant ship, low and heavy in the water, passed us going the other way. I thought about trying to swing across the water to their ship to hitch a ride back to Sam. But Fred had a better idea.

Just as the merchant ship passed, Fred kicked the top off the coffin, held it to his chest, and took a running dive overboard. He skipped on top of the water like a perfectly thrown flat rock. He paddled a few quick strokes, then stood up on the coffin lid as the curling wake of the merchant ship pushed it forward.

"Hang on, Sam. I'm surfing the Nile," hollered Fred. I let out a cheer.

The crocodile closed in. Sam backstroked and kicked away as fast as he could. Fred zoomed forward on the wake. An ugly green jaw full of teeth rose out of the water. Sam swam backward. Fred kicked his coffin surfboard forward.

Our captain took this moment to turn our boat. The sudden swerve knocked Thutmose and me off our feet. By the time we got back up, the only things I could see in the water were two pieces of well-chewed coffin lid.

I felt hot and cold and dizzy all at once.

Then I heard a familiar voice. "Ahoy, mateys, and cowabunga!" There was Fred, with one arm around a soggy-looking Sam. They had been picked up by the worker's ship following us and were standing safely on the deck. We saw the crocodile's head (with what looked like an extra lump) swimming for the safety of shore.

The captain brought our boat around, and picked up Sam and Fred.

"Most excellent sport and magic," said Thutmose. "You must show me how it is done."

"Sure, your highness," said Sam, giving Hatsnat his own version of the evil eye. "But this time we'll use Hatsnat for crocodile bait."

Hatsnat mumbled something about defiling the sacred resting place of the Pharaoh and excused himself, saying, "I must consult the signs of the heavens." Then he hurried off and made himself scarce for the rest of the voyage.

"I didn't know you could surf," I said to Fred.

"I didn't either," said Fred. "But I figured it couldn't be too different from skateboarding or snowboarding. Kind of like waterboarding."

"Thanks Fred," said Sam. "That crocodile never knew what hit him."

"That was nothing," said Fred, squeezing Sam in a headlock. "Besides, we wouldn't make a very good Time Warp Trio with only two guys."

Once everyone dried off, we enjoyed just cruising the Nile. The sun shone bright in a dark blue cloudless sky. The warm wind pushed us upstream. Thutmose proudly showed off everything built along the shore by his ancestors.

Fred scanned the horizon with one hand over his eyes. "So where are the great pyramids, the Sphinx, and all that stuff?"

Thutmose laughed and pointed back downstream. "About a week's journey that way."

Sam checked the sinking sun on our right and the river current flowing against us. "Of course. We're going with the wind and against the current. The delta and the Mediterranean are up north. We're headed south for the ancient capital, modern-day Luxor."

Fred squinted at Sam. "Of course."

We docked at Luxor just as the sun was going down. When we had studied Egypt in class, it seemed like this dusty, dry place with a few donkeys and pyramids and people walking around sideways like they're painted in those pictures. But the blazing sunset lit up a whole different scene.

Guys crawled all over the docks, yelling orders, throwing ropes, and tying up a hundred ships coming in. A million shops were crammed up and down the streets and a million shop owners were yelling what they had for sale. People walking all over the place made it look like the streets of New York at Christmastime, without the snow.

We were met at the dock by an army of royal attendants. I'm not sure exactly what we were expecting, but after hanging out and playing basketball with Thutmose, we had kind of gotten used to thinking of him as just another kid. The way everyone took care of him made us realize he was definitely not just another kid.

Servants laid out soft mats for Thutmose to walk on, shielded him from the setting sun with a huge canopy, and lifted him sitting on his throne into a gold and jeweled chariot.

Now I know what people mean when they say, "He got the royal treatment."

"He's like Michael Jordan, Elvis, and the president all rolled into one," said Fred.

"He's bigger than that," said Sam. "If you're a Pharaoh, you're a god on earth."

As new best friends of the god, we were treated pretty nicely ourselves. We got our own first-class chariot ride back to Thutmose's palace, where we were handed over to servants to clean us up for the Pharaoh's banquet.

We were pretty cool with the washing, massage, and putting robes on over our regular clothes. But then our servants started with the makeup, perfume, and jewelry.

"Wait a minute, wait a minute, wait . . . a . . . minute," said Fred. "I don't mind a little cologne, but I am not going to put on eye shadow. And that necklace just isn't me."

"With a face like yours, a little makeup couldn't hurt," said

Sam. "Besides haven't you ever heard the saying, 'When in Rome, do as the Romans'?"

"Everyone will be wearing this—men and women," I added.

"Number one, we are not in Rome," said Fred. "And number two, haven't you ever heard the saying, 'If everybody else jumped off the Brooklyn Bridge, would you too?'"

We finally talked Fred into a bracelet and a bit of black stuff around his eyes. Sam and I laced up our sneakers. Fred put on his Blue Jays cap, and we followed our guide into the banquet hall.

Hundreds of people were already there, eating, drinking, lounging around on benches and talking. Men and women were dressed in fancy pleated robes with twice as much jewelry and makeup as we had. Some of the women even had smelly cones of waxy stuff on their heads. No one gave us a second look. I wanted to find Thutmose and start figuring out a plan to find Anna and *The Book*, but Fred, as usual, had other ideas.

"Food! Look at that food!" The table in the center of the hall was piled high with roasted meats, fish, bread, fruits, and flowers. We followed Fred as he cut a path through the crowd to the food table. He grabbed a leg of roasted bird.

"Mmmm . . . duck. Or maybe goose." Another grab. "Bread. Mmmrph . . . a little chewy." Fred raised a green cup. "A little something to wash it down—woo! Wine."

"Fred," I whispered, pulling at his robe. "Take it easy. Let's try to act like very important guests, so we don't get into any more trouble."

Then we calmly and very importantly loaded our plates with roasted bird, figs, grapes, cucumbers, and bread. We finished that and came back for ox meat, more fruit, fish, nuts, and honey.

Sam wiped up the last bit of honey on his plate with a piece of bread and leaned back with a satisfied sigh. "I think I could get used to this."

Fred went back for one more helping of bread and ox meat. "That was just what I needed. All of that b-ball and surfing can make a guy hungry." Fred polished off the last of his custom-made ox burger and wiped his mouth on the sleeve of his robe. "Now let's get down to business and figure out how we're going to get out of here."

I looked around the room full of people still eating, drinking, and talking. "We're miles away from Hatshepsut's temple," I said. "I don't know how we're ever going to get back there to find Anna and *The Book*."

"No problem," said Fred. "We're friends of the Pharaoh. He can get us anything we want."

"I don't know," said Sam, pessimistic as always. "You know how our adventures usually turn out. I still can't believe we're in ancient Egypt and haven't been trapped in a pyramid or wrapped up like mummies with our vital organs in jars and our brains pulled out our noses with a hook."

"Thank you, Sam, for that pleasant thought," I said, scanning the room. I saw Hatsnat next to a pillar. He was with his whole crew of bald priests. "I have a feeling we've already run into the most dangerous thing in ancient Egypt. And we'll probably run into him again."

I was still trying to think of another good magic trick I could use to fool Hatsnat if I had to, when a blast of music quieted the room. A whole orchestra of musicians we hadn't seen struck up an official-sounding tune. Everyone stood up. A curtain at the far end of the room was whipped back and Thutmose and a very important-looking woman stepped forward. She was wearing an awesome cobra crown.

"Long live Hatshepsut and Thutmose," boomed a voice. "All hail!"

Everyone bowed. Thutmose and Hatshepsut took their seats at the head of a long table, and the orchestra started another tune. A line of girls clinking cymbals and clappers danced out from behind the curtain. My jaw dropped.

One of the girls looked different from the others. She had the same robes and makeup and instruments, but she was much paler. I stared at her and rubbed my eyes. She looked like Anna.

I looked again. She looked at me, then waved and smiled a familiar goofy little-sister smile.

EIGHT

"Anna!"

The girl danced over to us.

"Hi Joe. Isn't this all great?"

"But who . . . what . . . when . . . how did you get here?" I said.

"Oh, I met that nice lady with the crown that looks like a chair, just like the picture I showed Sam," said Anna.

"But that's Isis," said Sam.

Anna chimed her little finger cymbals. "Isis. Yeah, that was her name. She said I would meet you guys here, and you would need our help. So we sailed here on her boat."

"But Isis is a goddess," said Fred. "She wasn't real."

"That's not a very nice thing to say about someone," said Anna. "And she is so real. Otherwise—how did I get here?"

43

"This is getting stranger by the second," said Sam. "But before things get too strange, do you happen to have that *Book* you said had the picture of a woman with two Pharaoh crowns?"

Anna pressed her lips together in thought. "Hmmm. No. That's funny. Because right after I showed you that picture, everything twirled around and then Cleo and I were sitting in Isis's house. I don't remember what happened to the book."

"Oh no!" groaned Sam.

"Was it a library book?" asked Anna.

"Something like that," I said. "We have to find it before we go home."

"Well, we should just ask Isis," said Anna. "I'm sure she would help. She said—"

But before we could find out what Isis said, Thutmose stood up at the head of the table. Everyone was instantly quiet.

"Great Pharaoh, honored guests, tonight we are blessed by visitors from a land far, far away." Thutmose waved us up to stand next to him. He pointed to each of us in turn. "Sam, Joe, and Fred are from a land called America. Their people live in houses a hundred feet in the air and travel faster on the ground than any boat on the Nile."

44

The party goers oohed and ahhed.

Hatshepsut gave us that look you get from someone's mom the first time you meet her, when she's deciding if you are an okay friend for her kid, or one of those bad friends who will get her kid into trouble. I couldn't tell if we were getting the okay look or the bad look.

Thutmose took off a sneaker and held it up. "And they have shown me how to drive to the hoop and three-sixty slam with these magical sandals." More oohs and ahhs rose from the crowd.

Now we were definitely getting the "bad friend" look from Hatshepsut. I had to speak up and try to say something to make us look good. "We also use our magic sandals to . . . uhh . . . clean our rooms every day . . . very fast."

The mere mention of cleaning your room is usually enough to impress almost any adult. But the weird looks I got from Fred, Sam, and Hatshepsut let me know that this bit of news hadn't done much to make us look good. A familiar weasely voice piped up from the back of the room, and things went quickly from bad to worse.

"The magic sandals are very unusual," said Hatsnat, "and we are very interested that boys clean their rooms every day in America. But the priests of the temple and I have just one question for the three magicians."

"You want to know how to work the pick-and-roll play?" asked Fred.

"You guys need help on your three-point shots?" asked Sam.

Hatshepsut held up her royal hand for quiet. "What is it my priests wish to know?"

Hatsnat gave us that mean little smile of his, rubbed his bald head, and then dropped the bomb. "What were the three magicians from America doing inside the Pharaoh's treasure rooms?"

If you've ever seen your mom's face when she finds out something you didn't think she really needed to find out, you'll know what Hatshepsut's face looked like. "What is this?" She turned to Thutmose, who suddenly looked less like a god

and more like one of us. "You didn't tell me your new friends were found in my temple."

"Well, I . . . umm . . . didn't think you . . . ah . . ." mumbled Thutmose.

Some of the people in the crowd had begun to whisper to each other and shake their heads.

"They were found wearing and carrying your treasures, sire," added Hatsnat, obviously enjoying himself.

People whispered louder.

"And that one," Hatsnat pointed to Fred, "kicked a royal coffin and threw its lid to the beasts of the Nile."

The crowd let out a group gasp. Someone shouted, "No!"

"The signs we read from the stars tell us the Inundation is prevented by chaos among us. The signs we read say the chaos is these three."

I looked at Hatshepsut. Two thoughts crossed my mind. The first thought was: Isn't it amazing how little some things change? A person who is very mad 3,500 years ago looks just like a person who is very mad today. The second thought was: We are going to get our hands chopped off.

NINE

"Now just a minute," said Fred. "I had to use that lid to save Sam."

"So you admit it," said Hatsnat. "You threw the royal coffin lid into the Nile."

"Well yes," said Fred. "But we weren't stealing those treasures we were wearing."

"So you *were* wearing the Pharaoh's treasures," said Hatsnat. "That sounds like robbing to me."

The mention of that magic word sprung Sam into action. "We are not robbers."

"What are you?" said Hatsnat.

"Well . . ."

"What?"

The crowd looked from Sam to Hatsnat to Sam to Hatsnat like they were watching a tennis game.

"We are magicians, Hot Slop."

"Minions of Seth," said Hatsnat.

"Roasting Goober," said Sam.

"Temple thieves!"

"Steaming Greenie!"

"Hold it," said Hatshepsut, standing up. She spoke in a calm but commanding voice. "My high priest, Hatsnat, says you are the bringer of chaos and the cause of our drought. My nephew Thutmose says you are magicians. How do I decide which of these things is the truth?"

If you know any of the other Time Warp Trio's adventures, you know this is not the first time we've been in a spot like this. I saw it coming, and for once I was ready.

"Your Pharaoh-ness . . . sire . . . ma'am," I said to Hatshepsut, "if I may, I will demonstrate a bit of our magic to show the truth. I will match the strength of this young girl," I put my hand on Anna's head, "against any man you choose. If she is stronger, we tell the truth. If your man is stronger, Hatsnat tells the truth."

Sam turned absolutely white.

Hatshepsut thought about this for a second, then she nodded her cobra-crowned head, "That sounds fair to me. Thutmose, Hatsnat, agreed?"

"Sure," said Thutmose. "Maybe Joe will have her do the alley-oop."

49

Hatsnat didn't look so sure, but he fell right into my trap and picked his biggest priest. "Well, okay. But you must use Pepy."

Pepy was six feet tall, with shoulders three feet wide. I couldn't have picked a better victim myself.

"Perfect," I said, and went into action before anyone could change his mind. I stood Pepy on one side of me and Anna on the other, and put a hand on each of their shoulders. "Abracadabra, sis-boom-bah. Boom shaka laka laka, rah-rah-rah," I said in my most magical voice. "I have just taken the strength from this man and put it into this girl."

I placed a small wooden stool next to a wall and had Anna stand about three lengths of her foot away from the wall. "Keep your feet on the ground. Bend at your waist. And rest the top of your head against the wall." Anna leaned over. "Now place your hands under the stool, and lift it as you straighten up."

Sam closed his eyes and hid his hands under his armpits. "I can't watch."

Anna put her hands under the stool and stood up, lifting it with one easy motion. She smiled.

"Now Pepy must do the same," I said.

Hatsnat sneered. "Child's play."

Pepy stood three lengths of his foot away, leaned his head against the wall and . . . nothing. He couldn't budge.

"Now lift," said Hatsnat. "Stand up."

"I'm trying, your Excellency. But I cannot. Something holds me." Pepy tried again. Nothing.

"Step aside, you insect." Hatsnat whacked Pepy with his whip. "A little girl lifts that stool. Don't tell me you cannot."

Hatsnat stood over the stool, leaned his bald dome against the wall, grabbed the stool and . . . nothing.

"Urrgh."

Nothing.

"Ahhgh."

Nothing.

"Eeeeee."

Hatsnat stayed stuck to the wall. The stool stayed stuck to the floor. Hatshepsut looked amazed. "This little dancer lifts the same stool that the strongest man cannot budge? High Priest, this is magic. The gods have answered our question."

Hatsnat stood up. His entire head was dangerously red from effort and embarrassment. "Yes, your Worship." He gave a quick bow to Hatshepsut, then stormed out of the room. A line of nervous-looking bald priests followed him.

"Yes!" said Sam. "He shoots, he scores! Joe the Magnificent."

The orchestra started playing. The guests crowded around us, asking a million questions. Sam was happy to tell everyone about cars, jets, TV, phones, and music videos. Fred showed off his Blue Jays hat and demonstrated skateboard moves using a wooden serving tray. I gave Anna a quick hug. "Way to go, sis. You were great."

"Thanks," said Anna. "But I didn't do anything."

"I know," I said. "It works because of your center of gravity. Girls can do it. Guys can't. But you still did a great job." Out of the corner of my eye I saw Hatshepsut watching us. She was all smiles.

We had found Anna. Both Pharaohs were on our side. We were the life of an ancient Egyptian party. For the first time in my Time Warp life, I decided to relax and enjoy myself. We could worry about finding *The Book* later. What could possibly go wrong?

"I'm going to go get Cleo. I'll be right back," said Anna, and she skipped out the doorway the dancers had come in.

We laughed with the guests and told them about New York.

Ten minutes later, Anna wasn't back.

Some of the party guests said good-bye.

It was twenty minutes later, and Anna still wasn't back.

I checked out the doorway and up and down the nearby halls.

Thirty minutes had passed, and Anna still wasn't back.

I had a bad feeling that what could possibly go wrong had just definitely gone wrong.

TEN

When Hatshepsut found out that Anna was my sister and now she was missing, she ordered all of her people into action. Servants, dancers, musicians, and guests were given a part of the palace to search.

We looked in courtyards, pools, stables, gardens, and kitchens. We looked in bedrooms, bathrooms, servants' quarters, and hallways, storeroom jars, cattle pens, down the well, and even in the ovens. But there was no sign of Anna.

Fred, Sam, and I sat at the now empty banquet table with Hatshepsut and Thutmose.

"We've looked everywhere," said Thutmose. "Use your magic to find her."

"I wish," I said.

Hatshepsut took off her crown and rubbed her temples. "There is only one place in the palace we have not looked. Maybe Anna lost her way in the rooms of the Beautiful House."

"The Beautiful House," I said. "What's that?"

"Those are the secret rooms under the palace," said Hatshepsut. "It's where the priests prepare royal bodies for the afterlife."

"Oh no," said Sam. "Mummies."

"You mean taking out organs, packing with natron, opening the mouth?" asked Fred.

Hatshepsut looked at Fred in surprise. "American magicians know of our rituals?"

"Well, I did a diorama on it," said Fred. "So I learned a lot of stuff."

I was thinking about what Hatshepsut had said. Then everything suddenly made sense. "The people who use these rooms are the priests?"

Hatshepsut nodded.

"I smell a rat," said Fred.

"I smell a little bald guy with a whip," I said. "Can you show us the Beautiful House?"

"Only priests or members of the royal family can see those rooms," said Hatshepsut.

Sam looked relieved. I felt awful, thinking about Anna probably being held hostage by Hatsnat.

". . . but you must be priests to know so much about our rituals," said Hatshepsut. "Let's go."

Hatshepsut thanked all the guests and servants for helping us look for Anna. Then she got rid of everyone, equipped us all with torches, and led us down into the dark cool passages beneath the palace. We stopped at a fork in the long vaulted tunnel. Hatshepsut gave us our orders.

"The rooms to the left are where my departed husband, Thutmose II, was prepared to come forth again. I know those and will search there. The rooms to the left have not been used for ages. The four of you stay together and search there."

Sam raised his hand. "Um, don't you think we should all stay together? Because you know, this is what always happens in those horror movies. The group splits up and then people start getting bumped off one by one."

Hatshepsut gave Sam a funny look. "Horror movies? Bumped off? Let's just find Anna, then meet back here." She disappeared into the darkness of the tunnel and left Thutmose, Sam, Fred, and me nervously looking around.

"That Curse of the Mummy stuff was just made up for the movies," said Fred to no one in particular. "Mummies don't go around strangling people for real."

"Right," I said firmly.

"There are winged spirits, the *ba* of those here, who might not be happy. . . . " whispered Thutmose. He held up his torch to look in the shadows.

"Right," I said less firmly.

Sam groaned. "I told you this would happen."

"Knock it off," said Fred, pulling his hat down low on his forehead. "You guys are giving me the creeps. Hatshepsut said to search this side. So let's search." Fred walked down the tunnel, and we had no choice but to follow him.

We started out walking as close together as humanly possible. But as our eyes adjusted to the flickering torchlight, we began to check out the figures and hieroglyphs on the walls.

"Hey look," said Fred. "There's that dog-headed guy."

"Anubis," said Thutmose. "The god of mummi-fication."

"Of course," said Fred. "Good place for him, down here."

Sam held his torch up to the ceiling and lit up a figure that stretched all the way overhead and back down, her toes at the bottom of one wall,

her fingertips at the bottom of the other. "Nut," said Sam. "Goddess of the heavens."

We walked below the arched goddess and searched every nook and cranny for some sign of Anna. We must have looked in twenty different rooms. But Hatshepsut was right. They hadn't been used for ages. There was nothing in them.

"We're just about down to the end of these torches," said Fred. "We'd better get back to meet Hatshepsut."

I didn't want to leave, but we had searched everywhere. We headed back, hunting for any spot we might have overlooked.

I found a whole parade of gods walking along a wall we hadn't seen, and tried to remember who they all were. Thutmose supplied most of the answers.

"The bird-head man with the two crowns of Egypt."

"Horus, god of kings," said Thutmose proudly.

"The lady with a cow head?" I said.

"Hathor, goddess of love and beauty," said Thutmose.

"And who is this nasty-looking character?" said Fred, running his hand over a guy with a head that looked like an anteater with square ears.

"Seth," answered Thutmose. "God of chaos, brother and killer of—" He pointed to a figure holding a crook and flail crossed over his chest— "Osiris."

The mention of Osiris made me think of his sister, Isis, who had found the ripped-up pieces of him, put them back together, and brought him back to life. "Where is Isis? If anybody could help us, it would be her."

"Here," said Thutmose. "Right next to Osiris."

Sam's torch sputtered and went out.

"Our tour guide says the exhibits are closing. Time to get out of here while the lights are still on."

And I'm not sure why, but when I bent over to take one last look at Isis, I rubbed the ankh she held in her hand and said, "Isis." The raised bit of carved stone felt warm. I put my hand flat on the wall. The whole wall was warm.

I leaned against it and called to Fred, Sam, and Thutmose, already walking away down the tunnel. But I only got as far as, "Hey you guys. Feel this wall. It's—" Because when I leaned against the wall, the whole thing swung back like a giant stone door to reveal a hidden room. A fire burning in the corner fireplace lit up everything. I saw a pile of linen strips, a bunch of jars, a table covered with knives and hooked tools. A small mummy, half wrapped, lay in a plain sarcophagus. The mummy moved. I froze. The mummy groaned, then sat up.

ELEVEN

If my legs hadn't turned to rubber, I would have run the fastest hundred-yard dash ever, right out of there. But luckily, my legs weren't going anywhere. Because the mummy groaned again and said, "Hi, Joe. Have I been asleep long?"

"Anna!" I stumbled over to the little mummy in the sarcophagus. It was Anna. "What happened? Are you okay? We were looking all over for you."

Fred, Sam, and Thutmose piled into the secret room. Anna yawned again and stretched. A few strips of linen fell to the ground.

"Wow," said Fred. "Did you get turned into a mummy?"

"Yeah," said Sam. "She got her brain pulled out with the nose hook and now she's running on battery power."

"I must have taken a wrong turn coming back to the party with Cleo," said Anna. "I followed some lights to this room, but then the door shut and I couldn't get out. I was tired, so I lay down in this little bed with Cleo and used some of these covers. But now I'm all wrapped up." Cleo poked her head out from under the linen in Anna's lap, then made a big show of yawning, arching her back and stretching out her front paws. Thutmose patted her head and scratched under her chin.

"Thank Isis we found you," said Thutmose. "Hatshepsut was worried."

My torch gave a little sputter then died out.

"Uh, oh," said Fred. "We're running out of time." He stubbed his torch out on the floor, then handed it to Thutmose. "Here. You take the last two torches and go get Hatshepsut. When yours starts to go out, light mine. We'll get Anna free and wait here for you."

"With your magic sandals I'll be back in an eye blink," said Thutmose.

Fred dragged a stone block over against the

secret door to keep it from closing, and Thutmose ran down the hall, leaving us in the dim circle of light cast by the fire.

I started to unwrap Anna and noticed something strange. "Didn't you say you put these covers on yourself?" I asked.

"I was cold."

"But these are tied in knots."

"Hey," said Sam. He adjusted his glasses to study a stack of papyrus scrolls next to the fireplace. "Book of the Dead texts. Here's the whole scene of the Weighing of the Heart: Anubis checking the scale with the heart and the feather of truth, the Devourer waiting to chow down on any bad heart. It's just like my project scroll."

"Correction, Mr. Humble Genius," said Fred. "Your project scroll is just like this one. I think it beats you by a couple of thousand years."

"You know what I mean," said Sam.

"Do you mean what you say?" said Fred. "Or do you say what you mean?"

"I say you're mean," said Sam.

"Could you guys stop for just a minute and look at this?" I said. "Look at these knots."

"So?" said Fred. "They're knots."

"But Anna couldn't have tied these herself," I said. "So that means someone else has been in here, and someone else tied her up."

Sam checked out the knots and frowned. "Someone else like our old friend Hatsnat. He still wants to get rid of all of us because we know about his secret room."

Sam's words were chilling enough, but I felt a cool breeze from the doorway and turned to see an even more chilling sight. Hatsnat and four very large priests filled the doorway.

"Well said, my little magician," said Hatsnat. "And how nice of you to call me your 'old friend.'"

We stood frozen like statues. Even in the flickering firelight I could see Hatsnat's smarmy smile. He turned to his goons. "Wrap them up."

We put up a pretty good struggle. Fred got in a few excellent karate kicks. Sam did some furious toe stomping. Anna conked a guy on the head. And I almost escaped out the door, but got the wind knocked out of me by one of the monsters tackling me from behind.

In about five minutes we were right where Sam was afraid we were going to be—wrapped up like mummies, about to be buried alive.

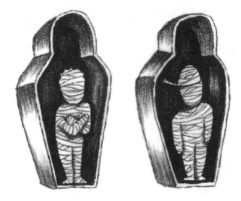

The muscle-bound priests propped us up in four sarcophagi leaning against the wall, then left the room. Hatsnat stood with one sandled foot against the stone block propping the door open. "I would love to stay and torture you for humiliating me in front of the Pharaoh, but I simply must run down the tunnel and tell Thutmose and Hatshepsut the terrible news."

"What terrible news?" said Sam. "That your real name is Earwax?"

"No." Hatsnat smiled grimly. "The terrible news that you accidently triggered the stone block that will seal this end of the tunnel forever."

"They won't believe that lame story," said Fred.

"There won't be any other story to believe," said Hatsnat. "Because no one will ever find you behind this mountain of stone." Hatsnat pointed above us.

"When they weigh your heart," said Sam, "it will be heavy enough with badness to feed the

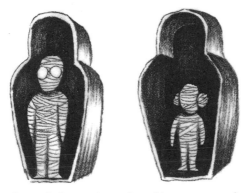

Devourer breakfast, lunch, dinner, *and* a bedtime snack."

Hatsnat paused like he was going to say something, then kicked the block away and swung the door shut with a heavy boom. We heard a few sharp blows of rock against rock. Somewhere overhead, stone slid against stone. Something bigger and noisier than five hundred subway trains rumbled above us. The whole world shook and fell, with one final gut-thudding *whump*. Then it was quiet, way too quiet.

A few wisps of dust floated under the door. The fire seemed to dim.

"I guess it wouldn't do much good to scream," said Fred from his sarcophagus.

"Nope," said Sam. "It would just use up our oxygen faster." The wedjet eye painted on his sarcophagus stared at me.

I thought about trying to wiggle free of the

wrappings and use the sticks of firewood to dig our way out, but I couldn't even wiggle my fingers. "I know this doesn't look good," I said, trying to sound positive. "But we'll think of something."

Fred wrestled with his wrappings. "Ooff. Like what? Taking turns breathing?"

Sam moaned. "It is really going to mess up my social studies grade if I croak and don't turn in my project. Joe, don't you know some Houdini magic escape trick?"

"We need more than a Houdini escape trick," I said. "If only I could have figured out how to hang on to *The Book*."

Anna stirred in her sarcophagus. "Can *The Book* help us get out of here?"

I tried to blink back the wrappings squashing down over my eyes. "Help us? It would have us out of here and sitting back in my room in a second."

"Well Isis told me if we ever got in trouble and needed her help to just ask," said Anna.

"She's delirious," said Sam. "Lack of oxygen. Talking about her imaginary friend again."

"We're completely tied up, trapped behind a million tons of stone, and all we have to do is ask a goddess who's not even here for help?" said Fred.

"Yes," said Anna.

"No way," said Sam and Fred in unison.

"You want to bet?" said Anna.

"Sure," said Sam. "What have we got to lose? Our coffins? I'll bet you a million dollars."

"Two million," said Fred.

"No," said Anna. "It has to be something you can pay. Like a week's allowance and a week of cat-litter-box cleaning."

"It's a bet," said Sam.

"It's a bet," said Fred.

"Okay," said Anna. "We really should pinky swear, but I'll have to trust you."

The fire dimmed even more. The feeling of being trapped under a mountain of rock started to weigh on me.

"Isis," said Anna, "please help us find *The Book*."

The firelight flickered. Somewhere a few loose pebbles fell. Then silence.

"That's it?" said Sam.

"Um, Isis," I said, "if you could work on the *Book* thing as fast as possible? We're kind of running out of time."

Deathly silence.

There was a scratching sound, and suddenly Cleo

was standing on the table. She sat down, looked at Anna, looked at me, then jumped down to the stack of papyrus scrolls Sam had been reading. I could just barely see her out of the corner of my eye. She was pawing away at the top of the stack.

And I can't be sure because of the bad light and weird angle, but something either fell down and opened up, or else Cleo pulled it down and opened it up. Either way, the thing that fell down was one beautiful blue book with twisting silver designs. And the green mist that rolled out when it opened was our ticket through 3,500 years to home.

TWELVE

Sam sat on my bed admiring Fred's ox-hide sandals. Every other trace of our Egyptian robes, jewelry, and makeup had somehow disappeared. "Nice," he said. "I think these could be the start of a whole new sneaker line—Air Thutmose III."

Fred turned his 'Making of the Mummy' diorama so it faced the wall. "I don't mind the sandals, but don't ever mention the word 'mummy' to me again. I get the willies just thinking about getting wrapped up like that."

"I wonder what happened when Thutmose came back with Hatshepsut," I said. I added the last of the new sugar-cube columns that turned King Tut's tomb into Hatshepsut's temple. "Do you think they believed Hatsnat's story?"

"I don't know," said Sam, rolling his Book of the Dead scroll. "I think they probably knew he did something sneaky. But I'll bet he did get away with making his secret room."

I leafed through my *Civilizations of Ancient Egypt* book. "It says here that Thutmose III was one of the most successful Pharaohs of ancient Egypt. They call him 'The Egyptian Napoleon.' But look at this. After Hatshepsut died, her statues were wrecked, and most monuments with her name were defaced. Some blame Thutmose, but they don't really know who did it."

"I'll give you three guesses what sneaky bald-headed priest did it," said Sam. "And the first two don't count."

There was a knock on my door. Sam hid the sandals under my bed. We all tried to look as innocent as possible. "Come in," I said.

The door swung open, and there stood Anna, cradling Cleo and Barbie in her arms. She held out her hand. "Allowance money please. Joe, you clean the litter box this week. Sam will clean next week. And Fred can clean the week after."

Fred and I dug in our pockets and handed over our cash. Sam just kept his arms folded. "You know—I don't think we really lost the bet, because it was Cleo who helped us, not Isis. I mean come on, she's a mythological figure. What proof do we have that it wasn't just a lucky accident? Maybe Cleo was just looking for her litter box and knocked down the papyrus where *The Book* was hidden."

Anna sat her Barbie down on my sugar-cube temple. "Maybe we could ask Isis to wrap you back up and bury you in that room for proof."

Sam looked at Anna. Cleo sat up in Anna's arms and gave Sam her full golden-eyes-wide, ears-up stare. Sam dug into his pocket as fast as he could.

"On the other hand, since it would be virtually impossible to recreate the exact circumstances for a valid scientific proof . . . I'll just give you the cash."

Anna smiled, tucked her handful of dollars in her jeans, and left.

Sam, Fred, and I looked at each other and shrugged.

And I don't know what look most Barbies have, but the one sitting on my sugar-cube model of Hatshepsut's temple is definitely smiling.

BONUS MATCHING QUIZ

Match the terms on the left
with the best description on the right.

1. Inundation

    A. Boy king who Joe thought was going to be in this book but isn't.

2. King Tut

    B. Goddess. Wife and sister of Osiris. Saver of Time Warp Trio.

3. *shaduf*

    C. Fred's basketball sneakers.

4. Thutmose III

    D. Season when the Nile floods its banks.

5. Hatshepsut

    E. A long pole with a bucket and a counterweight used to take water from the Nile.

6. Isis

    F. Boy king who could drive to the hoop and three-sixty jam. Also known as the Egyptian Napoleon.

7. magic sandals

    G. I'll bet you your allowance and a week of kitty-litter cleaning she was a Pharaoh.

74